The Bicycle with TWO Front Wheels

BY PIPPA REYNOLDS

ILLUSTRATED BY ANNA KRUCZYNSKA

AuthorHouse™ UK
1663 Liberty Drive
Bloomington, IN 47403 USA
www.authorhouse.co.uk
UK TFN: 0800 0148641 (Toll Free inside the UK)
UK Local: 02036 956322 (+44 20 3695 6322 from outside the UK)

This book is printed on acid-free paper.

ISBN: 978-1-6655-9468-4 (sc)
ISBN: 978-1-6655-9467-7 (e)

Print information available on the last page.

Published by AuthorHouse 02/26/2022

authorHOUSE®

The Bicycle with Two Front Wheels

Matthew, Ed, and Nick were brothers.

They lived in a big house with …

their dogs,

the budgie,

and their mum and dad.

The boys' mum and dad both went to work. It seemed as if Mum was at home when Dad was at work, and Dad was at home when Mum was at work.

When they were all together, they had a big family meal and sat around the big table in the kitchen.

Mum would say, "What's the best thing that happened today, and what's the worst thing that happened today?"

Nick was bored of this game and yawned, but he always joined in.

After supper, they usually argued about who would wash the dishes.

Everyone in the family liked different things.

Nick liked listening to music, watching films, and staying up late with his friends. His bedroom was always messy.

Matthew liked learning things, such as information about the football teams, the capital cities of countries, and the kings and queens of England.

Ed liked to be on the go and was always moving, especially with his football.

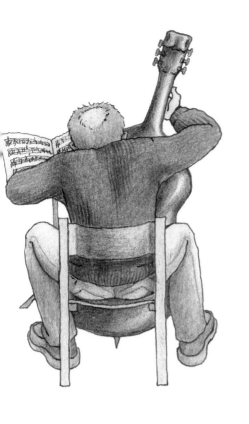

Dad liked playing his cello, walking the dogs, and making things in his workroom in the cellar.

Mum liked reading, mostly on the train, in the bath, and in her room. If she wasn't reading, she was chatting on the phone.

Life was busy, and after work, school, homework, and housework, these were the things they all liked to do.

One day Ed and Matthew came home from school. They grabbed some food and sat down to watch the cartoons on the television.

Mum came in, sat down, and said, "Dad and I aren't happy together, so we're going to try living in different houses. You will live half the time with me and half the time with Dad. We both love you, and we are very sorry this is happening. You haven't done anything wrong, so this is not your fault."

When Mum went out of the room, Ed and Matthew did not talk to each other but rushed upstairs to tell Nick.

Nick didn't seem surprised. They talked about Mum and Dad for a while, but before long they were talking about football.

In a funny way, life carried on just the same, but
everyone knew it was very different now.

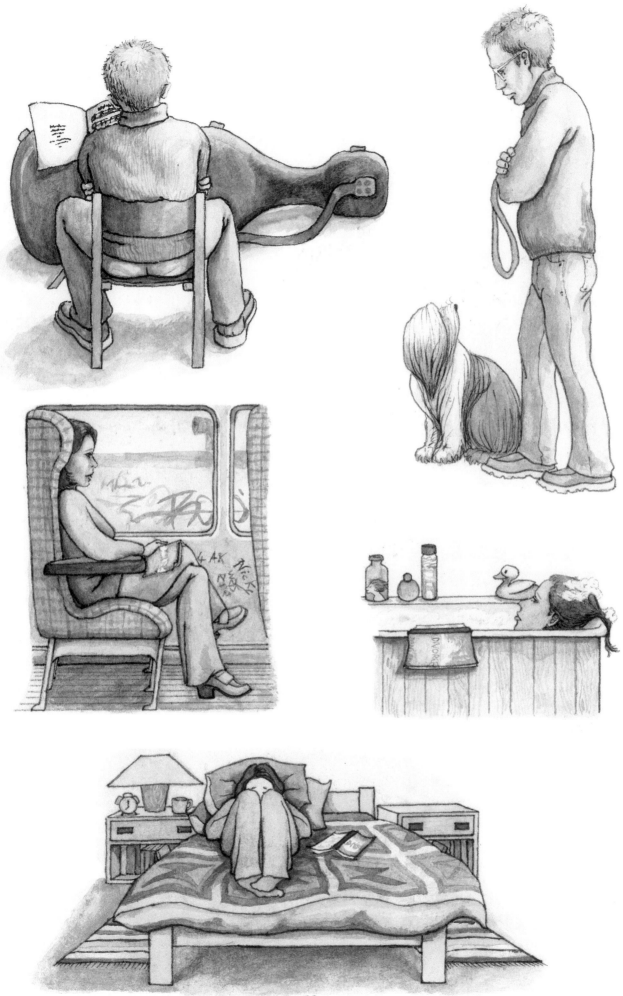

The weeks went by and turned into months. The day for Mum to buy her new, different house was getting closer. Everybody seemed quiet and sad, but nobody said very much.

Ed and Matthew slept in a bedroom right at the top of the house—the attic room. There was a window in the roof, so at night the boys looked straight up at the black sky.

Ed had started to wake up in the middle of the night. He didn't know why. He lay on his own, looking through the window in the roof. He would try to look for stars, but it seemed he could only ever see a black, starless night sky.

He didn't wake Matthew up. He just lay there wondering why he was awake.

It happened on Monday night,

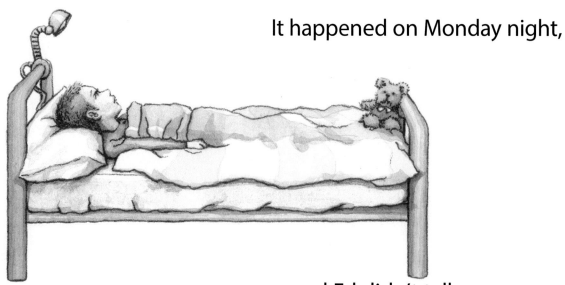

and Ed didn't tell anyone.

It happened on Tuesday,

and Ed didn't tell anyone.

It happened on Wednesday night,

and Ed still did not tell anyone.

It happened on Thursday night, and in the morning Ed told his mum.

'Hmm,' she said. She looked very thoughtful and confused. "If it happens again tonight, just come straight down to me."

"OK!" said Ed. He picked up his bag and went out the house and off to school.

On Friday he went to bed as normal, and deep in the night, long after he had gone to sleep, he woke up. Quietly but swiftly, he pulled back the covers, stepped out of bed, and made his way to his mum's room.

It was so dark and so quiet. He stepped over the dogs in the hall, and they didn't move—they were fast asleep. He pushed open the door to his mum's room and was surprised to see that she was awake, almost as if she were waiting for him.

She lifted back the covers and said, "In you get, then! Shall I get us some warm milk and biscuits?"

"Mmm!" said Ed.

They drank the milk and ate the biscuits. Ed knew this was very unusual—usually they couldn't eat in bed because they would have to brush their teeth again.

Mum asked him how he felt when he woke up in the middle of the night.

Ed thought, *A bit like I do before a football match—churned up in my stomach, like butterflies.*

"And what are you thinking about?" Mum asked.

"Nothing," said Ed.

"Well, have you got any pictures in your mind?" she asked.

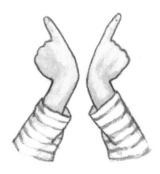

"Yes," he said, "I keep seeing a bike with two front wheels. The front wheels go like *that*," Ed said, making a V shape with his hands, "and I don't know how to ride the bike. I think I'll be OK just going straight, but I don't know how to go round corners because the wheels are going in opposite directions."

Mum listened hard. Eventually she said, "Do you think that the two front wheels going in opposite directions are a bit like Dad and me splitting up and going in different directions, and you're a bit scared about what will happen?"

"Yes ... yes ... it is a bit like that."

Mum carried on. "I feel scared too, because it's all going to be very different, and we can't really know what it will be like until we do it. Not knowing what it's going to be like is scary."

They talked for a while but gradually drifted back to sleep. It was strange, but from then on Ed stopped waking up in the middle of the night.

The day arrived for Mum to move into her new house. The removal men came and packed all Mum's stuff and half the boy's stuff—half their books and half their clothes.

Mum was very busy, and
Dad was very quiet.

By teatime Mum had opened the door to her new house, and the boys wanted to see what it was like.

It seemed very small and was a bit dirty.

"We'll have to decorate it," Mum said.

But it had a garden with grass so Ed could practice his kick-ups, and there was a boy next door, about the same age as Ed and Matthew, who was really friendly.

There was also a cat that came into the house and seemed to want to live with them.

"Nick was pleased to see that he had the biggest room, but then he was the biggest after all.

After a couple of days Mum had unpacked lots of boxes and had made the kitchen tidy so that they could sit down and have a meal together.

"Best and worst?" she asked and the boys talked about what had happened at school. Nick yawned but he managed to join in.

When the meal was finished, they had an argument about who was going to wash the dishes. In the evening they drew the curtains and watched the television for a while.

When it was late, Mum said, "Come on up to bed, and I'll read a story."

Ed and Matthew felt a bit funny in their new bedroom. They looked for a story to read, but their favourite one was in their other house, with their other books and toys, with their dad and their dogs. They missed them.

They settled for a different story, and while Mum was turning to the first page to start reading, they gazed out the window.

"It's a nice view," Matthew said. "You can see quite a lot from here." And they could—they could see the school playground, the top of the church, and lots of trees.

"You can see the stars!" Ed exclaimed.

Then Mum began to read. Not their favourite story, but a new one. A different story, and they were all wondering how it would turn out.

The End